For our mothers.
—*M.B. & C.R.*

To all *2000* of my friends and family members.
Sorry if I left anyone out.
—*J.B.*

THE 2000 YEAR OLD MAN
Goes to School

Mel Brooks & Carl Reiner

Illustrated by
James Bennett

A Byron Preiss Book

HarperCollinsPublishers

ABOUT FOUR DAYS AGO, *a plane landed in America with a man who claimed to be 2000 years old. Today, that man is visiting a school just like your own to tell the children of the world what it's like to be 2000 years old.*

...

Kids, this is your chance to ask the oldest man in the world anything you want.

Sir, are you *really* 2000 years old? It's hard to believe because nobody has ever lived more than 122 years.

I'm only 1999 ³/₄?! I'll be 2000 on October sixteenth!

How did you know how old you were back then? There were no calendars!

That's very true! Back in the old days, we didn't have formal years or days. Nobody kept time. We just sat around, pointing to the sky, saying, "Oooh! Hot! Whoa!" We didn't even know it was the sun!

What were your parents like?

My mother—she kept busy all day cleaning, cooking, and killing . . . mainly chickens. On Friday nights anything with feathers was a goner. That woman plucked till dawn. I don't remember much about my father. He was basically a quiet man, but strict. I can still hear him bark, "Candles out at seven!"

What did you use for transportation
back when you were a boy?

Mostly fear.

Fear transported you?

Fear, yes!
You see, an animal would growl at you, and you would
go two miles in a minute!

Did you have to work as a kid?

You mean like a job? Well, in those times there wasn't much work. As a kid, I was lucky to have one of the few jobs available. I would take a piece of wood and rub it and rub it, and clean it and hit the earth with it, and then hit a tree with it.

Why did you do that?

Just to keep busy! There was nothing to do! Absolutely nothing! Hitting a tree with a stick was a good job! Mostly people sat around looking at the sky. Another job you could get was watching each other. Just looking at each other . . . very popular.

What language did you speak?

We spoke rock, basic rock.

Could you give an example of that?

Yes. "Hey, don't throw that rock at me!
Put that rock away! Call the police!"

Where did you go to school?

Well, I went to primary, secondary, and high school. The primary school, what we called primitive school, was in an underground cave.

Secondary school was in an open cave,

and high school was on a cliff.

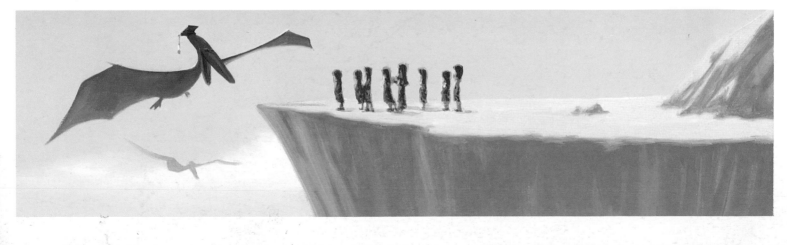

Which period of the school day did you like least?

Lunch! I hated lunchtime.

Most students today love lunch period.

Sure, because their parents pack them a nice peanut butter and jelly sandwich for lunch. WE had to first FIND our lunch! By the time we caught, killed, and cooked a wooly mammoth, lunchtime was over. We never got to eat.

Didn't they give you snacks?

2000 years ago, we ate only what was natural and organic. Clouds, stars, rocks! We ate big things and small things... like ants. But we had to be careful of the red ants because a few live ones on your tongue will eat your tongue before you eat them. You had to be very fast with red ants because it's more or less a race with them.

Did you go to college?

Who didn't? I was recruited by
Vesuvius University—the biggest
mistake of my life.

You didn't get good marks?

On the contrary, I got great marks!
I've still got them—on my back,
my arms, my shoulders—that rotten
Mt. Vesuvius erupted all over me.
I still have a headache from that
explosion!

Sir, I'd like to find out how some customs started.
For instance, singing. How did singing start?

Fear!

I thought you told us that fear started
transportation?

Songs came out of fear, too!

Can you give us an example?

How about the handshake, sir? How did that start?

Fear!

The handshake wasn't for friendship?

Back then, handshakes were a very tricky thing. A handshake was a way to see if a fellow had a rock or a dagger in his hand. You grabbed his hand! You held a hand, you looked and you opened it up, then you shook it. You had to find out if it had a STONE or a MARBLE that the other person could STICK IN YOUR EYE. That's the way the handshake started.

Sir, how did dancing start?

Fear.

Fear *again*?

Yes, FEAR! The only thing you could do with the handshake was to see if there was a rock or a rubber band or a marble or a nail or something they could stick in your eye, right? But you're only using one hand! Dancing is the COMPLETE use of BOTH hands, plus you keep the feet busy so the person can't kick you!

Sir, can you tell us something about how words got started? For example, how did the word *shower* originate?

Hmm, most words came about because of onomatopoeia.

You mean they sound like what they are?

Yes. You go to shower and you hear ssshhhhhh. Then you add hot water. You walk in,

ssshhhh OW

ssshhh OW er!

Let's take another word: *egg*.

You might think EGG doesn't sound like an EGG. Watch a chicken. Look at a chicken. Study a chicken very very closely as it produces an egg, and as you listen to it, you'll hear the chicken goes *eeeeeehhhhhgg*. Boo! An egg comes out.

Sir, you must know about some of the
legendary heroes who existed during
your lifetime. For instance, Robin Hood.
Was he real?

Lovely man. Ran
around in the forest.

Did he really steal from the rich and give to the poor?

He stole from EVERYBODY and kept EVERYTHING.
Who knew? He'd give you such a knock on the head when
his Merry Men robbed you flat, you wouldn't remember
anything anyway.

Did you know King Arthur and his Knights of the Round Table?

There was no ROUND Table. When Arthur ate with his family, it was a round table. When his knights came, he would open it up and put leaves in the table. So it was really King Arthur and the Knights of the OVAL Table.

Is it true in those days that the knights were so gallant they would fight for ladies' handkerchiefs?

Yes! A handkerchief was one of the big fights! To win a lady's handkerchief, two knights would go at each other on horsies with long spears, you know? They would run at each other to get at the handkerchief.

Why?

Because they hadn't invented TISSUES yet! Once a knight got that handkerchief, he would blow his nose pretty good.

Sir, did you know William Shakespeare?

Oh, what a pussycat! That little beard, that cute hair!

Was he the greatest writer of all time?

Shakespeare was NOT a great writer. Not a good writer at all! He was a DREADFUL writer.

But he wrote thirty-seven of the greatest works ever!

Yes, but did you ever see his handwriting? A blotch of ink with an L looked like a T, an M you didn't know was an M, an O could've been a P, an S looked like an F. Every letter was cockeyed and crazy. Don't tell me he was a good writer! He had the worst penmanship I ever saw in my life.

Sir, which great explorers or inventors do you feel were most important? Columbus? Einstein?

Einstein was good. He was good.

But who do you personally feel was one of the greatest contributors to our civilization?

Murray . . . Murray was a fabulous inventor. He invented fire. He was standing under a tree when a big bolt of lightning set the tree on fire. It set Murray's beard and his clothes and his hair on fire. He came running into the cave, all on fire, and I jumped up. I remember I leapt to my feet and I said to everybody in the cave, "Get your marshmallows on your sticks!" And then we all rushed at Murray, but we were so greedy, we put him out. Too many marshmallows put Murray out.

What has kept you alive for all these years?

Will Tolive.

Well, children, the *will to live* has kept many people alive. I'm sure that's what our guest means.

No, dummy! Not the "will to live." Dr. Will Tolive. William Tolive has kept me alive for the last twenty-five years. A genius, the man's a genius. He told me to do everything slowly. Never, ever run for a bus! There'll always be another. He also told me to eat fruits. Fruits are the elixir of life. There's a fruit for any disease that mankind has had.

What about diarrhea?

For diarrhea you gotta eat peaches.

Peaches. Any kind of peaches?

Oh, no, not Alberta.

Oh, really?

No, you must have the CLING peaches.

Why?

They hold you together a little better!

One last question, sir.

OK, but that's it. I gotta sit down. My feet are killing me.

Do you remember any of your teachers?

Yes. Mrs. Weinstein. She was the oldest teacher in the school. We called her "Mrs. Redwood." She taught for four hundred years. She was so old that her father was a Neanderthal. In the winter, she wore him to class.

What was your homework like back then?

It was HOMEwork. Literally. We had to build a home. In wood shop they gave us logs. We had to saw them up, take them away, and put up a house. No house, no graduation! Boy oh boy, did we do our homework so we had a place to sleep. Very smart principal.

Grade

D

Before you leave, sir, any advice to my students based on your $1999^{3}/_{4}$ years?

Yes. Don't listen to hip-hop when you are doing your math homework! It'll mess up your brain.

That's it?

Oh, yes: Never, ever put a candy bar in your pants pocket!

That's *all*?

OK! OK! Come closer so you can hear this, children: Don't cheat! When you take a test, never copy from another student's paper because the person that you are copying from could be dumber than you!

Well, kids, I've got to take off.

The 2000 Year Old Man Goes to School   Text copyright © 2005 by Brooksfilms Limited and Clear Productions, Inc.   Illustrations copyright © 2005 by Brooksfilms Limited, Clear Productions, Inc. and Byron Preiss Visual Publications, Inc.   Hear more of the wit, wisdom and life lessons of the 2000 Year Old Man—pick up *The Complete 2000 Year Old Man*, four hilarious CDs, available from Rhino Records at a record store near you or via www.rhino.com   Special thanks to Jake Forrestal, Ali LoConte, Erica Morreale, Christopher Morrissey, Matt Muller, McKayla Muller, William O'Connor, and Mary Beth Rogers for lending their voices to the audio recording.   Printed in the U.S.A. All rights reserved. No part of this book may be used or reproduced in any manner whatsoever without written permission except in the case of brief quotations embodied in critical articles and reviews. For information address HarperCollins Children's Books, a division of HarperCollins Publishers, 1350 Avenue of the Americas, New York, NY 10019.   www.harperchildrens.com

Library of Congress Cataloging-in-Publication Data   Brooks, Mel.   The 2000 year old man goes to school / by Mel Brooks and Carl Reiner ; illustrated by James Bennett.—1st ed   p.   cm. Summary: A 2000-year-old-man visits an elementary school and answers questions from a teacher and students, such as "Did you have to work as a kid?," "What language did you speak?," and "What has kept you alive for all these years?"   ISBN 0-06-076676-X — ISBN 0-06-076677-8 (lib. bdg.)   [1. Prehistoric peoples—Fiction.   2. Old age—Fiction.   3. Schools—Fiction. 4. Humorous stories.]   I. Title: Two thousand year old man goes to school.   II. Reiner, Carl, date.   III. Bennett, James, ill.   IV. Title.   PZ7.B7976Aae   2005   [E]—dc22   2004015696 Typography by Martha Rago   1 2 3 4 5 6 7 8 9 10   ❖   First Edition